S.M. FLANAGAN

Wedding Values

This edition first published in paperback by
Michael Terence Publishing in 2022
www.mtp.agency

Copyright © 2022 S.M. Flanagan

S.M. Flanagan has asserted the right to be identified as
the author of this work in accordance with the
Copyright, Designs and Patents Act 1988

ISBN 9781800944763

No part of this publication may be reproduced, stored
in a retrieval system, or transmitted, in any form or
by any means, electronic, mechanical, photocopying,
recording or otherwise, without the prior
permission of the publisher

Cover image
Copyright © ZzzDim
www.123rf.com

Cover design
Copyright © 2022 Michael Terence Publishing

Contents

Chapter 1:
Wedding Photography 1

Chapter 2:
A Shocking End to a Relationship 3

Chapter 3:
Pete Questions his Future... 5

Chapter 4:
At the Function, the Wedding Photography..................... 10

Chapter 5:
Pete's Wedding Contemplation.. 15

Chapter 6:
Pete Alone with his Mother 18

Chapter 7:
Another Wedding Session (Wedding Photography) 20

Chapter 8:
Pete Spent Time with his Mother 22

Chapter 9:
Wedding Bliss.. 25

Chapter 10:
Regression 27

Chapter 11:
Wedding and a Long Journey Home................................. 30

Chapter 12:
Sweet Times with Mike and his Wife 32

Chapter 13:
Bridal Suite Talk 35

Chapter 14:
The Photographer and the Bride 37

Chapter 15:
The Photographer's Last Time with Amy 40

Chapter 16:
One of the Best Highlights of the Photographer's
Experience 42

Chapter 17:
Pete's Reflection on Past Weddings and Wedding
Photography 45

Chapter 18:
Pete's Deep Thoughts 47

Chapter 19:
The Photographer's Pictures 49

Chapter 20:
Friday Night 51

Chapter 21:
The Dream Model (a Former Bridesmaid) 53

Wedding Memories 56

Wedding Reflection 57

The Photographer's Deep Wedding Memories - and
Reflection 59

Chapter 1:
Wedding Photography

Pete Hamley attended a wedding. That day the professional wedding Photographer took photographs of the wedding. These photographs consisted of wedding guests, newlyweds, wedding celebrations and wonderful romantic imagery of the wedding itself at the church, reception and country manor in its fine gardens.

The beautiful wedding photographs photographed were very fine.

That Wedding Day consisted of the wedding, reception and time allocated for the wedding Photographer to take photographs. The Photographer had a good day. These photographs captured the wedded couple's bliss and all those well-wishers and wedding guests celebrating and everybody else having a good time that day.

This wonderful wedding was special and truly memorable. Of course, this was one of the experienced Photographer's best times as a Photographer.

In the wedding Photographer's photography, he captured great bliss and joy from the newlyweds and those invited guests celebrating.

That day the wedding Photographer spent time doing his wedding photography.

The Photographer had such a great time. Having such a great experience. This ranked as one of his best experiences and one of his best days as a wedding Photographer taking exclusive photographs. That day, everything went remarkably swimmingly.

Chapter 2:
A Shocking End to a Relationship

Pete came in to see Sally, his girlfriend. At that time Sally did not want to see him. Sally was unconcerned and indifferent towards Pete. Sally was rude and impolite towards her boyfriend.

"Go! Get out!" shouted Sally.

Pete did not expect this outburst from Sally. Pete stayed calm. Wondering why Sally remained moody, hostile, nasty and unpleasant towards him. Pete could not understand Sally's behaviour which was appallingly bad.

"What's wrong with you?"

Sally explained her feelings.

"It's over. It's over between us. Can't you see? It was never going to work out. Our relationship is not working out. Get out!"

Pete suggested a compromise.

"Can we be friends?"

Sally rejected the idea.

"NO! It's over. I don't want to see you again."

Pete intended to have a motive.

"Don't you want to see me?"

Sally objected to seeing Pete.

"NO. I don't. Get out!" yelled Sally.

"It's you. You're the one who is unreasonable. You are the problem."

Sitting on a settee gracefully, Sally picked up a soft cushion and threw it hard near Pete who was standing opposite, slouching ungracefully. In a hurry, Pete left the house at once. He had a nervous disposition. He never intended to return there ever again. His once passionate emotional relationship had come to an end.

Pete hated Sally. He unloved her. He split up with his girlfriend. Pete never really understood fully the trouble of his ill-fated relationship.

Sally, now an ex-girlfriend, seemed quite relieved at how she had broken up with her boyfriend. Sally felt pleased and relieved that their relationship was now over. Their short relationship only lasted several months.

Driving home by car, Pete reached home. Late at night, Pete stayed downstairs in the lounge. He sat in the armchair for hours. At this time, he felt sad, miserable and deeply upset yet again. He stayed downstairs for hours. Sitting in the comfortable armchair. He nodded off in the dark. Pete slept for hours. Finally going to bed in the middle of the night, Pete had a nightmare!

Chapter 3:
Pete Questions his Future

One autumn evening, Pete sat with his relaxed and cheerful Mother in the sitting room. It was quieter there than anywhere else in the other downstairs rooms. The spacious room warmed up from a radiator. They took comfort from the central heating. The sybarites enjoyed the luxury of it.

Pete cooled down by being in another room. It was cooler and darker in there. There the luxurious sitting room was furnished with a suite. He still hadn't overcome his setback which he had expected to happen. He preferred to be alone, to reflect on today's wedding photography at the autumn wedding. But his Mother intruded on her son. Invading his privacy. Expecting her son to tell her of his disappointment. His misery was made worse by being pent up. Sally disappointed him with her immediate response to her rejection. Pete felt deeply disappointed, unhappy and miserable and could not overcome his disappointment.

From a lamp stand, a light was on in the sitting room. There it was cooler, darker and shadowy. The light reflected in the shadowy, dark room. It cast shadows. The house lights shone everywhere else including the garden where the radiant light radiated.

"Son. What's the matter? You can tell me."

With embarrassment the son confirmed,

"I have split up with Sally."

"It wasn't ever going to work out, was it?" scowled Mother.

"I guess not."

"What will you do?"

"I'll keep working. Keep doing my wedding photography."

"You do have your wedding values!" remarked Mother.

"Oh! I do. A wedding is supposed to be the best time of one's life! I like to make it memorable with all the good photography of the wedding. For a long time, couples will remember their unforgettable day."

Wanting to know, the Mother asked the question,

"Tell me. What happened? How did it come to this?"

"Mom. I don't know. I haven't seen Sally for days. I think Sally had enough of me. Me not seeing her. Sally decided enough was enough."

"Can you blame her?"

"I guess I can't. I am too committed to my work. I don't have time to see her. It's getting difficult and hard with all my travelling and photography," said son honestly.

"It's such a pity. You loved her. Did you?"

Pete deep with emotion remained too upset. He

could not cope with disappointment. His feeling of deep unhappiness and sadness. He could not come to terms with his grief.

Answering the question,

"Really. I don't think I'll ever get over it. At being jilted like that."

"Never mind," consoled Mother. "It may be the best thing. You could do a lot better."

"I suppose I could. Love is not cheap," said son unhappily.

"What will you do?" asked Mother.

The son answered honestly.

"Keep working. Keep doing my good photography. My job is to take good photographs. The finer the photographs, the better it will be."

The Mother observed her downcast son.

"Aren't you down?" asked Mother.

"I am down. I will get over it," answered son.

"Have you taken any good wedding photographs lately?" asked Mother.

"Oh! Yes! Those beautiful Bridesmaids photographed together with the Bride." replied son.

"Was that a pleasant experience for you?"

"Oh! Indeed. You learn new things every day. Even the slightest difference is an experience. Everything new. The Bridesmaids are photogenic. They look good. The virgins are beautiful!" said son frankly.

"They will grow up. Then of course they will get married themselves."

"I should think so. Who would be the lucky man?"

"What's the main thing happening in the photographs?" enquired Mother.

The emotional son expressed his emotion.

"It's the newlyweds first. They get all of the photographer's attention. Then it could be the wedding guests and families next. Or either the Bridesmaids. The virgins could be divine and special. Yeah! The way they move and stand still gracefully. Hold bouquets and the Bride's wedding dress. How every Bridesmaid looks good. Looking beautiful. They are special. I am amazed at them," said son candidly.

"How long will you be a wedding photographer, from now on?"

"As long as the job lasts me. The company employs me."

Suddenly Pete picked up a camera from the settee which he had left there inadvertently. The son took a photograph of his exuberant Mother. The Mother who felt tipsy and inhibited objected to her picture being taken. The Mother raised objections to being photographed. The Mother ran her fingers through her hair. It was a peroxide ginger.

"Don't! My hair."

The son was exasperated with his Mother who stretched out her arms in objectional disapproval. The Mother refused to have any more pictures taken by her son.

"Put it away! No more!" objected Mother.

Getting up and going upstairs to his tidy bedroom, Pete was well-pleased with the photographs he had taken with his camera many hours earlier today. He seemed self-satisfied. Getting personal contentment was his most motivational purpose of all.

Chapter 4:
At the Function, the Wedding Photography

Pete attended the wedding at the church. The photographer took photographs of the wedding guests who gathered together at the church.

The photographer also took wedding photographs of the married couple standing with members of their families and three Bridesmaids standing together as they held bouquets. They looked really beautiful wearing peach dresses.

Later the wedding photographer attended a wedding reception where he took beautiful photographs of the newlyweds out in the Manor House gardens. The grounds were incredibly lovely. Beautifully landscaped with natural features.

The Professional Wedding Photographer was being polite, pleasant and friendly. He somehow got them to stand together in the right position to pose for the camera which was on a tripod. They struck up an attitude. The Females looked beautifully Feminine dressed up when standing, holding bouquets and posies. Posing for the camera. The Photographer was too absorbed in his work to pay attention to anyone. An extroverted Bridesmaid came up to the distracted Photographer. The pretty Bridesmaid sought his attention. Wanting desperately to talk to the Photographer. The Bridesmaid was fascinated by the professionalism of the Photographer. The Bridesmaid had the desire to be a model to be photographed. The act of modelling compelled her. She had an obsessive interest and fascination for the Photographer. The other two luscious Bridesmaids looked on. Wondering if she would get an acknowledged response from the Photographer. Their eyes and pouted lips were sultry. With grace, they stood gracefully together.

Pressing for an answer. The Bridesmaid prompted the Photographer.

"Can you take a picture of me?" asked Ann.

The amused Photographer looked at the extrovert. Having a deep respect for the gorgeous Bridesmaid.

The Photographer reminded her of the situation and of the situational complexities.

"Your name is Ann. I believe I have already taken a picture of you. You are included in the photography," answered Photographer.

"I want to be a model. I want to be photographed," insisted Bridesmaid.

"You can be a model. You really can. Not now. Perhaps when you are older. Now is not the time," said Photographer dogmatically.

With girlish childishness, the Bridesmaid spoke. Declaring her willingness to be a model.

"Can I? I really want."

"You will make a good model. You do have what it takes. You're a natural," remarked Photographer.

The Bridesmaid gestured. Pointing a finger. "How about them?"

"They are good. They are photogenic."

The newlyweds looked on. Wishing them the best. The married couple were full of concern for them. Neither of them engaged in a conversation. Both Husband and Wife were beatific.

"Do you have any weddings to go to?" asked Bridesmaid.

"I do. I am fully booked," replied Photographer.

With interest, the Bridesmaid did wonder.

"What did you think of the wedding today?" asked Bridesmaid.

"I have had a good day," smiled Photographer.

With regard to the Bridesmaid's sentiment, she expressed it.

"I am third time lucky," exclaimed Bridesmaid sweetly.

"You are. Are you?"

"You see I wanted to be a Bridesmaid at two other weddings. But unfortunately, I was rejected. My aspiration to be a Bridesmaid just didn't happen. My hopes were dashed," added Bridesmaid.

The Photographer had sympathy for the Bridesmaid.

He was quite sympathetic towards her. The Photographer adored the Bridesmaid. He marvelled at the virgin.

"You're sweet. So adorable. How can you not be a Bridesmaid? You are a natural!"

For the Photographer, meeting Ann had been his highlight of the day at the wedding. Ann a lovely Bridesmaid had got the same limelight too. Just like the newlyweds did. Husband and Wife got overjoyed and overexcited.

After the Photographer's photography session had finished, the overjoyed and rejoicing Bridesmaid took the opportunity to say and wave goodbye to the Photographer packing up and leaving. The adoring Photographer adored the sweet Bridesmaid. He had such a deep love and admiration and adoration for Ann. The Photographer was overworked during this photo session. The coy Photographer grew fond of Ann. He liked her. Ann was a beautiful Bridesmaid. A stunning Blonde. Her golden-Blondeness was beautiful!

Ann was irresistibly appealing and alluring. An irresistible Bridesmaid! He did wish he could see her again! Pete felt deeply sad as he embarked on his long journey home.

As Pete reached home, he found his Mother waiting for him in the luxurious Lounge.

Feeling weary and exhausted. He sat down in an armchair, sitting opposite his Mother on the other side of the room.

"Well. Tell me. How was your day?" asked Mother.

"I had a wonderful day. It was marvellous. I met an Angel!" said son coyly.

"Well. What happened?"

"I encouraged her to model. I was encouraging. I didn't want to discourage her and be negative," said son honestly.

"That's awfully good of you," smiled Mother.

"I shall really miss her. It was a great experience," said son sadly.

Chapter 5:
Pete's Wedding Contemplation

Pete came into the dining room. There he saw his youngest Brother sitting on a dining chair at the dining table doing his studies. He disturbed his brother deep in thought. Concentrating on studying.

"What are you studying?" asked Brother.

"What is Morality?" asked the younger Brother.

"Is that religious?"

Ian distracted from doing his work turned and faced his Brother.

"Yep. Your job is glamorous. There is glamour at weddings. Now, tell me. What do you think the meaning of life is?"

Pete thought of the philosophical question asked.

"The fundamental factor is from my personal experience. Yes. There is the religious aspect of it. The spiritual and the fleshly. Also, the worldly and the materialism. I believe it's all about ethics and ideologies."

Ian understood the principle.

"To me, it seems to be about being successful. Trying to do well in modern British society. That's what it appears to be," said Ian.

"Yes. I do get it. Take my job for instance. It is about glamour and wedding bliss. To do wedding photographs. The wedding photography does consist of the wedded couple, wedding guests, and wedding imagery of Bridal – and flower arrangement," said Brother.

"It's wedding glamour, romance and honeymoon," remarked Ian.

Pete made comments about it. He undisclosed the photographic process.

"Of course, weddings are supposed to be the best times of people's lives. Indeed, the photographs are a good memory of it. It does remind them of the wedding."

Ian observed his Brother. His sad look. Realising he had been disconsolate. His disconsolateness was a result of being saddened.

"You look down," said Brother.

Pete acknowledged with a sad response.

"I am indeed. I saw something special. It just slipped away."

"What do you mean exactly?" asked Brother.

Pete feeling sad preferred not to say. He kept quiet about it. Otherwise, he did intend to blab out. He remained reticent.

"I would rather not say. It hurts me," said Pete reticently.

"Don't talk to me if it's personal," grumbled Brother.

Pete wanting to be alone left his Brother to study. He stayed in his bedroom to rest. Earlier today he developed a negative in a dark room.

Chapter 6:
Pete Alone with his Mother

In the Living Room Pete and his Mother sat by a fireplace. They both kept warm from the fire. Warming up when sitting at opposite corners. They both enjoyed having a cup of tea. In the glow of the firelight. From the fireplace, they were enchanted by the sight of the glowing light.

"How was work today?" asked Mother.

"I had a really good day. My sessions went well. I met some interesting people. I took some great photographs of the wedding. The Bride looked beautiful. I captured her beauty on camera. I took some fine photos."

"Is it all glamour?" wondered Mother.

Pete spoke with honesty.

"Weddings can be glamorous. It is glamour. At the wedding, I take photographs. I like to make people happy. To remind them of their memories. That's the beauty of photography. Husband and Wife are blissful. They are together with their happy families and wedding guests. The Honeymooners go on their romantic honeymoon. Going on their Honeymoon can be the best days of their lives."

"I read an article about failed marriages. One in three

marriages end up in divorce," mentioned Mother.

"Hey! That's common. I only see the happy side of it. Happy weddings. It doesn't cross my mind. I do expect their marriage to work out. I only deal with photography at weddings. Weddings are a great bliss. A time of happiness. Bride and Groom wed. I take photos of them and their families and wedding guests. I take it at church. At a place somewhere else. Usually at a wedding reception and a glamorous venue. Hopefully, the wedding photos keep their memories alive."

"Son. Will you tie the knot?" asked Mother.

"Crikey! No! I have split up with my girlfriend. It is unlikely," said son assuredly.

The Mother took pity on her son.

"Oh! It's a shame."

"Since I have been jilted, I haven't stopped crying," exaggerated son.

The Mother got up and walked to the other side, to a corner where her son sat uncomfortably. The son rose and stood up in expected anticipation of his Mother. The Mother threw her arms around her son. The Mother hugged passionately her son.

"My Boy!" exclaimed Mother childishly.

The son reacted passionately by hugging his Mother. They both cherished their loving togetherness. Son and Mother had deep love for each other. It was a passionate hug. In the glow of the firelight, an enchanting glow in the flickering light.

Chapter 7:
Another Wedding Session (Wedding Photography)

Going to another wedding, the Photographer was already prepared for photography today. The Bride and Groom wed. The American Bride's family were millionaires.

At the church, the flower arrangements looked beautiful and everything else was prepared for the wedding. This lovely wedding was glamorous. A glamorous one! The slick Photographer organised and arranged the wedding guests into positions so that he could take wedding photographs of them gathered together. Subsequently, after the wedding at the church, the busy Photographer took wedding photographs of the newlyweds. Hence the new Husband and Wife were beatific. This included their families, joining in the wedding photography and subsequent wedding celebrations!

The Photographer attended the function, a wedding reception only for a short time. This wedding session was scheduled. The Photographer took only some wedding photographs. At a venue, the professional Photographer took photographs of the wedded couple out in the beautiful grounds and gardens of a Country Manor House. The Photographer beautifully photographed them. The Photographer did not dither at any of his wedding sessions. Every session had been productive photography. As a professional, he was business-like, organised and uncommunicative. His uncommunicativeness a silence.

So ended another photography session at a wedding.

Today it was a romantic, glamorous wedding at a historic venue. The wedding Photographer took wonderful photographs at a romantic location in a historic attraction. It was a glamorous wedding!

Chapter 8:
Pete Spent Time with his Mother

Due to financial commitments, both son and Mother had gone to work. The Mother worked for a Bridal suite and shop and her son worked as a Freelance Photographer.

Later that Friday night, son and Mother spent time together in the living room by a fire. Keeping warm in the comfort of the luxurious room. They both had an ordinary conversation.

"Son, why don't you get married?" suggested Mother.

The son appeared to be uninterested in marriage. He was uncommitted about getting married.

"I can't. It's over between me and my girlfriend," replied son.

Unashamed the Mother made her remark,

"You do have problems making friends and having relationships."

The son admitted his failing.

"I don't doubt that. I am a photographer. I take wedding photographs. For general photography, I organise and arrange how I want things to be done. How people pose for the camera. Their stance. I make my decision. I am in control. I have the power in photography."

"You do, son. You do," paused Mother. "Why don't you get married and settle down?"

"No, Mother. Things just won't work out."

"I am concerned for you. I do fret. Isn't it awful? Son, I really want you to be happy," wished Mother.

"Yes, Mom. I am dedicated to my job, and to my photography. Nothing else seems to matter."

"Son. That's good. You have dedication," said Mother proudly.

The son did have motivational and dedicated values.

"I do love photography. It's my life. It's my occupation."

"Do be competitive which you are. Don't settle for anything less," urged Mother.

"Mom. I shan't," assured son. "I shall do my best."

"I will keep working at the Bridal suite. It is good work," smiled Mother.

The son thought of his Mother's joy at being beneficially complimentary to his occupation. A common interest of theirs. Pete became tired and left his Mother.

Alone downstairs, very late at night, Pete went

straight to bed to sleep.

Shortly afterwards, his Mother came upstairs to go to her bedroom. His Mother got into bed for her beauty sleep.

Chapter 9:
Wedding Bliss

Pete attended his friend's wedding. Pete was one of the wedding guests at a wedding ceremony at church. He sat in a pew with all the other wedding guests sitting there in the rows of pews.

The Reverend conducted a wedding ceremony. The Bride and Groom took their vows. Pete a photographer been assigned to wedding photography today. Every session was split into three. Pete did a favour for his friend. In the first session, the photographer took photographs of the wedding guests at the church, gathering together. Followed by the photographer who took wedding photographs of the newlyweds posing together with members of their families and Bridesmaids.

During the afternoon, all of the wedding guests attended a wedding banquet at the church hall.

Pete stayed for the banquet then later he took wedding photographs of the newlyweds, their families and wedding guests. The overworked photographer ended his last and final photography session by taking photographs of the newlyweds out in the church gardens, in the churchyard. Standing there posing together, the Husband and Wife were blissful and euphoric. The wedded couple had such joy of married bliss. Within an hour, the married couple went away on their exotic Honeymoon. The romantic Honeymooners were beatific when taking their honeymoon in the Indian Islands.

Their Honeymoon was unforgettable.

Pete had an enjoyable time taking the wedding photographs at his friend's wedding.

The good memory of it was quite memorable. His good friend a married man had an unforgettable time at his wonderful wedding. He was madly in love with his wife!

Chapter 10:

Regression

Pete's Mother came home from weekly shopping. The son waited for his Mother in the living room, in restful relaxation. His tired Mother sat down and relaxed in an armchair. His Mother lounged in comfort, enjoying the luxuries, indulging in eating luxury chocolates, caviar with crackers and drinking sherry.

"What was the highlight of your friend's wedding?" munched Mother.

"Actually, seeing my friend getting married was an experience. I am so used to being a wedding photographer. It was strange. Everybody was so nice to me. There was so much love. I appreciated it. I was appreciative of their love. I touched them all. Thanking them all. All the well-wishers too. I was happy for their love. I was so sad because I wouldn't see them again. From my departure, I missed them all. Now it's a memory of mine," recalled son.

"Oh, what a shame. What was the best thing about the wedding?" asked Mother.

The son took note of his friend's wedding.

"Seeing the joy and happiness at the wedding. It was great. What an amazing experience," answered son.

"You don't disclose much about it. You don't say

much how about you feel."

"I keep it confidential. I don't want anyone to know how I feel."

"Are marriages a joy and bliss?"

"They are. You get good, bad and indifferent marriages as well as marriages of convenience. I have had disappointing relationships. For me, doing my photography is a consolation. I have got joy and satisfaction from doing it. It's a pleasure to work with people. It's one of the best things about it. Weddings can be shrine-like. For instance, the beautiful Bridesmaids and Bride. Then there's the photography. Capturing the wedding beauty. It's glamour and glory. Do weddings live up to one's expectations? I believe they do. The Honeymoon itself is fulfilling. A joyous experience. A blissful Honeymoon. The lovers walk hand in hand. The Honeymooners are deeply in love! At the time of their Honeymoon," said son happily.

"Are Honeymooners fulfilled on their Honeymoon?" asked Mother.

The son did not fully answer the question. "Some are. Some not. The nature of weddings is beautiful. I am having a fabulous time at weddings. It's wonderful. Everybody else does too," responded son.

Pete lost enthusiastic interest in talking to his Mother now. The son got up and left his moody Mother a depressive! His Mother was a divorcee.

Pete opened the sliding patio door with tinted glass. He stepped outside. Going outdoors in a large garden.

Pete sat down on a garden chair. There sitting out in the shady shade and breezy air. He felt electrified by the nature of beauty. Its natural glory. Pete cooled down when sitting in the shade. Enjoying his privacy as well as the peace and quiet out here in the lovely garden. He stayed out in the garden for a long time. In deep contemplation, he had been philosophical, spiritual and regenerative. His prospects were optimistic. The photographer regressed and regenerated. He had been sullen, regretful, wistful and pensive.

Chapter 11:
Wedding and a Long Journey Home

Pete usually declined invitations to weddings (with the exception of friends' and families' weddings).

At times, Pete envied the Brides and Grooms. Either they were too successful, handsome or beautiful and that included the virginal Bridesmaids. He envied how they were beatific and deeply in love. As a wedding photographer, he was accustomed to weddings. (Declining invitations to other people's weddings.)

His job was normally to take wedding photographs. These photographs consisted of newlyweds, their families and wedding guests.

Pete experienced weddings as happiness. He had empathy for the newlyweds. How their Wedding and Honeymoon could be a climax or anti-climax. He got also used to the idea of glamorous weddings and glamour weddings. Also, the marriage was bliss and joy.

The wedding photographer normally did his job at weddings. The photographer photographed at every wedding session.

The venues depended on location at the church, at the wedding reception and glamorous locations in beautiful England.

Normally the photographer was assigned to a wedding. He had finished every photography session. Then straightaway he left the wedding to depart, subsequently to make his journey home.

Coming home, Pete avoided his family. He stayed in his bedroom where he rested for hours alone in bed. Pete a Bachelor desired a wife! His desire was a wild fantasy! He took glory in being a Bachelor!

Chapter 12:
Sweet Times with Mike and his Wife

Pete came to Mike's house. Mike was a friend of his. A fellow Photographer. He ended up spending the night at Mike's house. They both had a late-night tea and a long conversation. This time without Mike's wife being present. Pete made a complimentary remark.

"It's amazing. I have seen the transformation in your life. You have done well for yourself," remarked Pete.

"It's been a pleasure knowing you. Things have worked out well," said Mike happily.

"You're one of the best Photographers I have worked with," complimented Pete.

Mike underestimated Pete's ability.

"You are a good Photographer. You really are," paused Mike. "I have heard you have split up with your girlfriend."

Pete felt embarrassed at the rumours spreading. Every rumour was an embarrassment.

"My relationship just didn't work out. It was inevitable how it ended."

"What a shame. I hope you find someone. You do

meet beautiful women. That's a good thing."

"I guess it's a good thing. It's a consolation being a fine photographer," boasted Pete.

"You make the Brides' lives a joy. Don't forget it," said Mike.

"And not forgetting the Bridesmaids. What such joy they are. Such beautiful virgins," praised Pete.

"They are special without a doubt," remarked Mike.

On a joyful note, Pete thought of it.

"I get great pleasure from being a photographer. The Brides, Bridesmaids are the best thing about it."

"The amount of photography I have taken of them. It's unbelievable," said Mike proudly.

With proud joy Pete was thrilled.

"Over the years I have taken some great photography," said Pete proudly.

Pete took a photo album which Mike passed him to look at. Curiously Pete looked through a photo album. He admired the beautiful photographs in a photo album. Mike's attractive wife was voluptuous and natural. The wife was photogenic. The wedding photos of the Bride and Groom with the lovely Bridesmaids posing with them. These were adorable and lovable. These Bridesmaids looked naturally angelic with platonic great love. Their expressive expression revealed that. Their natural countenance and disposition.

Having enough of midnight talk Pete left Mike with

his sweet wife. Pete went to bed after midnight. Quite strangely he dreamt that night. His sweet dream was electrifyingly thrilling.

Chapter 13:
Bridal Suite Talk

Pete sat in a Bridal suite with his Mother. Pete spent time alone with his Mother. They both enjoyed their time of privacy at being together. He thought of how Brides spent their time in the luxury Bridal suite.

Pete experienced the sensational wonder of it. He did have empathy with Brides intending to wed there.

"What is your average routine of being a wedding photographer?" asked Mother.

"It's all about preparation. The actual travelling is the main thing. Getting to a destination. Regarding wedding photography, I do sessions. Taking quality photographs of wedding guests and wedded couples in a church or a lovely location. A seclusion, retreat. Weddings are bliss and joy. It can be a glamorous wedding and glamorous. As soon as I have done my sessions of wedding photography I can depart. Weddings can be glamorous and glamour at times. Weddings are very expensive. It can be a Female affair. You have the Hen night and Stag night but that is something entirely different which is not related to weddings. The key to a photographer's success is his preparation. Then there are the travelling and photography sessions. When it's done the photographer makes his departure. The wedding photography is of high quality. From memory, one remembers their Wedding Day. Isn't it lovely!"

answered son.

"I still remember mine," said Mother.

His Mother locked up the premises. Leaving the luxurious Bridal Suite. They both made their way to a parked car. Mother and son got in a car. The son drove his Mother, a passenger back home. It was a short journey back.

Chapter 14:
The Photographer and the Bride

On Wednesday afternoon Pete met a romantically in love Bride at a Bridal suite. The romantic Bride was looking forward to her wedding on Saturday. Amy was in love and romanticised as she dreamt about her wedding and marriage.

The Photographer expected to meet Amy. The impatient Bride anticipated his arrival.

His Mother insisted to her son that he should take the time to reassure Amy and offer her advice. Amy was an independent young Englishwoman and deeply in love with her intended. The Bride looked into her compact mirror.

"Do I look alright?" she asked anxiously.

"You look fine. I shouldn't worry. You look good," reassured the Photographer.

Amy ran her fingers through her hair.

"How about my hair? My makeup?"

"Don't worry. You will look fine," he assured her.

"I do hope I have a happy wedding," worried Amy.

"Amy- that's your name, isn't it? You will be fine. I shouldn't worry. Everything will be alright on the day."

Amy had some concerns and doubts about the

photography. She appeared to be doubtful regarding this photograph. The Bride apparently was camera shy.

"Will my photos be alright?"

"Oh! Yes. The photos will turn out well. Don't worry. The Photographer will do that," replied Photographer.

"Will you be taking my photos?" enquired Amy.

"Yes, I will. I am doing your wedding photography," confirmed Photographer.

The Bride seemed pleased with the sessional arrangement of wedding photography.

"Oh! God! Will it be alright?"

"Yes, of course, it will be alright. There is nothing to worry about."

The Wedding Photographer was assigned to Amy's wedding. The Photographer looked at the attractive Bride with such a sweet charm and nice personality. The thoughtful Photographer reassured the anxious Bride who was becoming negative.

"You look good. Your photos are natural. You have such a sweet smile. It's a charm," remarked Photographer.

"How about my makeup?" fussed Amy.

"Don't use too much makeup. Don't overdo it. You do have a natural look. You'll be fine," advised Photographer.

As soon as someone else intruded on them, the Bride stood and thanked the Photographer. Amy with deep emotion said goodbye to the emotional Photographer before leaving the Bridal Suite. Amy had no intention of returning to the Bridal Suite. Time was running out. Amy had less than two days before her glamorous wedding.

Pete went home. The next day he made final preparations for his wedding photography. The Photographer put new film in his camera. He adjusted the lens of his camera accordingly. In accordance with any technical adjustments, his camera required.

On the Wedding Day, Amy was beatific. Amy favoured the Photographer with deep appreciative love and joyous appreciation.

Amy felt obliged to the charming Photographer.

Amy's wedding remained memorable.

Chapter 15:
The Photographer's Last Time with Amy

During midweek, the Photographer went to the Bridal Suite. The Photographer expected to see Amy a married woman. Amy entered to see Pete's Mother. Amy expressed her thanks. The Photographer expectedly saw Amy for a short time. Amy stayed only for a short time at the Bridal Suite. Amy had been superstitious as she returned to the Bridal Suite. Amy had such good memories of there. Amy was romantically sentimental about the Bridal Suite.

The conversation between the Photographer and the married woman was a short one.

"I shan't stay long. I just wanted to say thank you. I'd like to thank you for your wedding photographs. They are lovely. I had a wonderful wedding day, as did my Husband, friends and families," thanked Amy.

"It's a pleasure," smiled Photographer.

"I was wondering. As a Photographer, what's the most frequent question Females ask you?"

"They ask me how do I become a model? The Females do ask me. They enquire about it. They get put off. They lose heart. As a Photographer, I encourage modelling. I am not accommodating. I do weddings. I am not a fashion Photographer," stated Photographer.

Amy lost heart in modelling. Amy had an apathy for it. She felt apathetic about it. Amy was utterly demoralised at becoming a model! Amy left the Bridal Suite immediately. Amy never, ever returned there again.

Chapter 16:
One of the Best Highlights of the Photographer's Experience

The Photographer arrived late at the wedding reception. Earlier, he had a preparatory initiative regarding sessional photography.

Attending the wedding reception to which the Photographer had been invited. The venue was a grand Country Manor in the loveliest garden. All the wedding guests sat at tables, set out in an incredibly lovely garden. A beautiful one.

All of the tables were laid with luxury tablecloths and set with fine silver cutlery, table napkins and candlesticks with lit candles. The mahogany furniture was of fine quality.

According to the Photographer, this wedding reception seemed strange. The wedding guests invited were all females. The women wore beautiful evening dresses and gowns. The ladies were chic, elegant, cosmopolitan and cultured. The Photographer who came out into the garden observed them. He was overwhelmed at the sight of the lovely Ladies who dined. All of the wedding guests dined on seafood in marinated sauce. This particular wedding was glamorous. A glamour one.

Wedding Values

All of the attractive women looked lovelier and prettier dressed up glamorously.

The Photographer was assigned to this wedding. A wedding photography session. Subsequently, at the end of the wedding, the Photographer did not work at this time.

With wonder, he was greatly overwhelmed by what he experienced. He was stunned by the lovely, dressed-up female wedding guests. At this time, he expected them to dine. The Photographer looked at the loveliest women in admiration. He marvelled at their beauty. Admiring them. The attractive ones were sexier, voluptuous and curvaceous.

A few women were stunningly photogenic. The beautifully dressed women, the female wedding guests looked appealing, irresistible and enticingly alluring.

Full of admiration, the Photographer had been tempted to take photographs with his camera. Finally, in his best interest, he decided that no photography should be taken. On this occasion, the joyful and elated Photographer experienced great joy. His experience was a memorable one!

The Photographer witnessed great bliss, happiness and joy from every wedding guest present there who dined out in the loveliest garden of a glamour location.

Due to superstition and subsequent intrusion, the distracted Photographer decided not to take any photographs of them. The Photographer left all of them to dine in peace rather than intrude on them by taking photographs.

All of the seated wedding guests and diners were exuberant, cheerful, merry and so happy.

Chapter 17: Pete's Reflection on Past Weddings and Wedding Photography

Pete came home from work. He rested with his Mother. Sitting in comfort, he warmed up in the lounge.

"My son. You have had a great career as a Photographer. You have been a Photographer for many years now. What is the secret of your success?"

Pete had a photographic contemplation. He had a deep reflection on past weddings.

"I love photography. I have a passion for photography. It is my job. In my time I have met many interesting people. From glamorous to ordinary to common. Weddings vary from time to time. My job is to take photographs to make people happy. From Bride and Groom. To Husband and Wife. To Mr and Mrs. Most couples' expectations of marriage are fulfilled. Some others may be unfulfilled. Maybe their Honeymoon is an anti-climax. Generally, married couples are blissful. That's what I like to see. Then my job has been done well. I get satisfaction and pleasure from being a professional Wedding Photographer. I have done the photography well. It is a memory. It is splendid my photography. I look forward to my next wedding. As a result of being a Photographer. My memories of weddings are wonderful and bittersweet. I can't complain. I love it anyway," paused son. "How can one get married? Isn't being a Bachelor the best thing? There are beautiful virgins. I won't go into that."

Suddenly the doorbell chimed. His Mother left the lounge to answer the front door. His Mother went out with her friend tonight.

In the meantime, Pete rested alone in the lounge. He relaxed while sitting in an armchair with his legs stretched out. Within a short time, Pete nodded off in a dark room. Thereafter the light turned into darkness.

Despite Pete's unhappy relationships with certain individuals, he still found solace and got a consolation from being a top wedding Photographer. Pete did his photography at weddings. It gave him consolatory satisfaction. Pete remained a Bachelor.

Chapter 18:
Pete's Deep Thoughts

Today Pete had a day off from work. He stayed in the lounge and rested on the settee. He took comfort from luxuriousness. The Mother came in and intruded on her son.

"Are you not working today?" asked Mother.

"No. Not today. It's my day off."

"I was looking at my magazines. What do you think is the finest thing about weddings?"

"Well. I specifically do my photography myself. Well, there is the Bride, the Bridesmaids, the children and of course all of the wedding guests. I also love the lovely locations and venues. I love the glamour of it. Married couples do love my wedding photography. To them, it is personal and sentimental. They do recall their wedding day with joy and fondness. Me doing the photography. I would like to be remembered for that. You work at the Bridal Suite. So, you really ought to know about it. You should have experience and knowledge of it," replied son.

"I do, son. I do. It's something I don't really talk about," said Mother coyly.

The Mother left her son alone to attend to his Grandmother. The Granny was mellow and wise.

Alone, Pete dozed off on the comfortable settee. He took comfort from luxury. Pete enjoyed his privacy. His time all alone.

Chapter 19:
The Photographer's Pictures

Pete and Mike both stayed together in the Living Room at Mike's home. Mike's wife wasn't present that night. Both Pete and Mike had an educational conversation about photography (Pete's photographic material of the Bride, Groom and Bridesmaids, excluding and including members of families).

"I do love your photography. It is so good," remarked Mike.

"What do you like about it?" asked Pete.

"That's a good question. I have actually seen your recent wedding photography. I do like it."

"What is it you like about it?" repeated Pete.

"Oh! I like the beautiful Bride and the handsome Groom. I love the gorgeous Bridesmaids. This photograph of the three Bridesmaids is marvellous and special. I like the angelic look. Aren't the virgins beautiful? This is what makes wedding photography special and unique. Also meeting the wedding guests is special too. The wedding can be glamour and glamorous. It's held in really beautiful locations."

"I quite agree. Weddings are wonderful. It is a memorable time. An unforgettable one," gasped Pete.

"Weddings too can be ordinary and commonplace.

Certain weddings have been like this. Such is the life of a wedding photographer," sighed Mike.

Mike, a photographer, showed photographs of his photogenic wife to Pete. Mike fussed over them. Looking at every photograph. Pete admired these photographs of his flamboyant wife. The photographer took these photographs well. A naturally atmospheric setting of mountainous scenery in the Alps. Its photographically scenic mountains.

"Your wife looks natural. Your photos have turned out well," remarked Pete.

They both relaxed together in a dimly lit room. A dim light. They both engaged in a conversation of a photographic nature. Pete expressed his preference for fashion photography rather than glamour photography.

Chapter 20:
Friday Night

On a nice spring day, Pete and his Mother sat in a summer house somewhere in the garden. The breezy air was cool. All of the trees blossomed in spring. They smelled the fragrant scent in the air.

Pete spent more time with his beloved Mother than on previous days. The son loved his Mother more than ever. He was convinced that without his Mother's support and financial backing, he would not have succeeded as a professional Photographer.

With favourable appreciation, the son favoured his Mother. Regarding his Mother, he had the utmost respect and regard for her.

Sitting on the corner of a bench. The dreamy Mother was deeply reflective.

"Now that you're spending more time with me, what is the best thing about weddings, would you say?" enquired Mother.

"Of course, being with you, Mom makes me happy," admitted son.

The happy Mother put her arms around her son. Squeezing him vigorously. The Mother felt deep passionate emotion.

"To me, the most important things in a wedding are

many. I am used to it. There is the flower arranging and lighting. The beautiful wedding dresses. The Bride, Groom, Bridesmaids, children and all of the wedding guests. Of course, the function. The catering and beautiful wedding cake. A glass of Champagne. The glamour wedding and the glamorous. As a Photographer, I concentrate on wedding photography itself. It's my responsibility. It has to be done to high standards. The photography can be taken at lovely locations and venues. Some weddings are good. I have been to wonderful weddings. I have had the pleasure and privilege of attending the finest weddings. Taking wedding photography. I do hope married couples like my photography. Generally, I am proud of my photography. I have pride. If it's done well. Then I am satisfied with my work," responded son.

Feeling the nippy air, Pete and his Mother got up and they both walked back to the detached house, going indoors. In the meantime, back at the house, his parents engaged in a typical romantic conversation.

Pete stayed in the study. He sat down on the swivel chair. He reclined on the desk. He relaxed in the silence of the study. He thought of the glamour wedding this Saturday. He took the initiative in his wedding photography session. The actual planning of the sessional schedule. He contemplated a glamorous wedding at the weekend.

With preparatory anticipation for the wedding tomorrow morning.

Chapter 21: The Dream Model (a Former Bridesmaid)

Mrs Brenner came to see Pete's Mother at the Bridal Suite. After Mrs Brenner's brief visit to the Bridal Suite, she stayed until Pete popped in. The photographer expected to meet Mrs Brenner.

Mrs Brenner appeared to be disappointed. Mrs Brenner had a deep concern for her Daughter. Mrs Brenner desperately wanted her Daughter to be a model. She spoke to the concerned photographer.

"Will you please help me? I want my Daughter, Monica, to be a model. She has the qualities of a model," said Mrs Brenner desperately.

The photographer remembered the past.

"Yes, if I remember, your Daughter was once a beautiful Bridesmaid at a wedding. Where I was the photographer. Leave it with me. I will see what I can do," assured Photographer.

Mrs Brenner lit up. Mrs Brenner became obliged. Wondering if the considerate photographer would do a favour with obligational intentness.

Mrs Brenner wanted a positive result. Mrs Brenner personally thanked the photographer for his consideration in negotiating with a top Modelling Agency.

Finally, weeks later the Modelling Agency accepted Monica Brenner as a Model. Mrs Brenner was overjoyed and rejoiced at her Daughter being accepted at a Modelling Agency.

Mrs Brenner was so pleased and very happy at present.

One day, Monica Brenner came to see the photographer at his home. Expecting Monica, he invited her in. The photographer welcomed her. (The lovely teenage Bridesmaid was once photographed at a wedding by Pete the Photographer, who was assigned to that particular wedding.)

The photographer led an excited Monica into a room. Monica expressed her appreciation.

"I just wanted to see you. I wanted to thank you for all that you have done for me," said Monica appreciatively.

"It's nothing. You're welcome," gestured Photographer.

"Do you remember? I was once a Bridesmaid at a wedding. You were the photographer."

The photographer expressed a deep sentiment.

"So you said. You were third time lucky."

"Yes, I was. It was a dream wedding. I was a dream Bridesmaid!" said Monica modestly.

Remembering the wedding. He recalled that the photographer was amazed at the teenage stunner. The stunning tanned Bridesmaid smelt of a beautiful fragrance. Her suntanned figure was curvaceous.

Suddenly the landline rang. The hurried Photographer showed Monica out of the house. At once Monica left the photographer's home. Monica full of delight had rejoiced. Monica was overwhelmed with such joy and happiness when making her way back home.

Wedding Memories

At one wedding, the Photographer's highlight that day was taking the wedding photographs of a handsome Bride and gorgeous Bridesmaids. These three were pubescent teenage Virgins. On that wedding day, the newlyweds got all the limelight at their wedding. The beatific newlyweds got the attention of everybody, including the wedding guests. The wedding guests were deeply fond of them. They deeply loved them. Showing the deepest respect. Having high regard for them. The married couples reflected on their weddings. They looked at their wedding photographs admiringly and with such joy. Their recollection of their wedding was a happy memory. A joyous occasion. The photographer was greatly happy and pleased at having been a part of it. At photographing them. The Photographer's memory of this romantic and glamorous wedding was a good one! Looking back at this wedding, in particular, nothing else could compare to the Virgins. The beauty of the virgin Bride and Bridesmaids beautifully dressed up. The Photographer was so proud of this wedding photograph. It remains one of his best wedding photographs. One of his favourite photographs of natural virgins and Bridesmaids at a wedding. The picture is so naturally good.

Wedding Reflection

On a fine summer day, Pete came out into the garden. There he joined his relaxed and restful Mother. The son sat next to his Mother on a garden chair. The heterosexual Photographer was an admirer of beautiful Brides and a connoisseur.

"Son, are you fulfilled as a photographer?" asked Mother.

"Oh. Yes. I have found fulfilment as a photographer. I love photography. I have a passion for it. Taking great photos is what it's all about. Over the years, I have taken so much photography. Taking wedding photography is what gives me pleasure. I love what I do. I take some fine photos. I get the chance to meet interesting people. I go to the finest country weddings. My wedding photos capture the beauty of it. The glorious wedding day. As a photographer, I do wedding photography. It's a specialist. I provide a service."

"You do indeed," nodded Mother. "My Son you are unmarried. Do you have any regrets about not being married?"

"I like being single and unattached. I like the freedom. I like being alone. I love being a photographer. I am an experienced wedding photographer. My photography of weddings is wonderful. It is special and unique. It is the memorable highlight of one's wedding," said son proudly.

The Son took pride in being a wedding photographer. He engaged in deep reflectional photographic contemplation.

The Photographer's Deep Wedding Memories - and Reflection

Pete was by himself in the back garden, standing and facing the direct shining sun. His eyes were blinded by the sun's rays. The sunshine was blazing and dazzling. The blaze blinded him. He averted his eyes from the glare. Pete reflected on his deep memories and past experiences as a professional wedding photographer. He had some good memories of past weddings. Now, he looked forward to summertime. He hoped this summer would be far better than last summer. He wanted something of a challenge, something more rewarding and satisfying. He fantasised about the perfect wedding. The most perfect wedding photography. This time the photographer was eager to undertake more wedding photography this season, in summer. Sessional photography which the wedding photographer was assigned to at weddings.

Mrs Brenner and her Daughter and a former Bride, a married woman came to the wedding suite. The relaxed and calm photographer expected to meet them. Both Mrs Brenner and her Daughter expressed their heartfelt gratitude.

"Thank you so much for what you have done for my

Daughter. Thank you."

"I am pleased that I could have helped you," replied Photographer.

Monica Brenner was deeply obliged to the Photographer, expressing her thanks. "THANK YOU SO MUCH."

Also, the married woman offered her thanks. Actually, having a deep appreciation and love for the photographer.

Recalling that wedding, he remembered the beautiful Bride and Bridesmaid. Both Virgins were gorgeous. The photographer doing his wedding photography had been overwhelmed by the gorgeousness of the curvaceous, virgin Bride and Bridesmaid. Naturally, of course, the photographer had never seen beautiful virgins, beauties quite so remarkably extraordinary and special. The photographer's deep experience was touching. This remained the highlight of the wedding and the wedding photographer's deepest memory. The photographer remembered how the adored newlyweds received all the limelight on their wedding day. They all cherished the occasion. Personally, thanking the photographer for his excellence in photography and for doing personal favours for them. With pleasure from fulfilment in photography, the photographer expressed himself.

"It was a real pleasure doing your photography. It does remain a highlight for me personally. I still remember it well," he said fondly.

The photographer's passionately emotional

encounter with Mrs Brenner and her Daughter and married woman, a former Bride was deeply moving and touching.

- THE END -

*Available worldwide from
Amazon and all good bookstores*

www.mtp.agency

www.facebook.com/mtp.agency

@mtp_agency